For Jon-Jo with love
M.I.

This edition is published and
distributed exclusively by
Discovery Toys, Inc., Martinez, CA

First published 1989 by
Walker Books Ltd., London

© 1989 Mick Inkpen

Printed in Italy

ISBN 0-939979-40-3

Jojo's Revenge!

Written and illustrated by
MICK INKPEN

DISCOVERY TOYS, INC.

Like all babies Jojo
was squeezed and
squashed and passed
around a lot.
Like pass the parcel.

Everyone wanted to
prod him to make
him smile.
Or poke their fingers
into his mouth to
see if he had grown
any teeth.

People would knit him
sweaters that were
too big.
Or too small.
The silliest one had a
matching pom-pom hat
with ear flaps.

And though his crib
was full of furry
animals, the things
he really wanted
were always out
of reach.

At night, just as Jojo was beginning to enjoy a good yell, someone would always find a way to stop him.

And once, even
his mom got cross
with him for filling
his diaper.
"Oh Jojo," she said,
"not now!"

So one day, to get back, Jojo decided that instead of eating his dinner, he would wear it!

After this there was
no stopping him.
Every day Jojo managed
to try on his breakfast,
his lunch and his dinner.
"It's because he's like
me," said Grandpa.
"He's artistic!"

Jojo's mom bought
him some face
paints to play with.
But Jojo ignored them.
He preferred to paint
with cereal.

Then one day Jojo's mom went out, leaving his grandpa to look after him. "Try not to let him make too much mess with his dinner," she said.

When she got back
she was amazed.
Jojo's plate was empty
and there was not a
single scrap of food
on him.
"Grandpa! How did
you do it?" she said.

"Like this!"
said Jojo's grandpa.